Alice and Dinah
New Tales from Wonderland

The Cheshire Cat's Surprise

Alice woke up one morning and said to Dinah,
'I wish it was my birthday.'

Dinah was busy. She was chasing a ball of wool round and round the room.

'Birthday parties are such fun,' said Alice. 'There are presents and music and party clothes and games to play and birthday cake to eat. But it's SUCH a long time till my next birthday. I wish I knew someone with a birthday today.'

Dinah stopped chasing the ball of wool and started to meow very loudly.

'I think we should go to Wonderland,' said Alice. 'Someone there is sure to be having a birthday party today.'

meeooou

Alice and Dinah jumped into the rabbit hole which leads to Wonderland.

Shrieking with laughter,
they fell faster
and faster.

Alice and Dinah landed together with a BUMP!

In front of them were two strange boys dressed in identical clothes. The boys were holding on to a large baby's rattle and refusing to let go.

'We're Tweedledum and Tweedledee,' they said together. 'Who are you?'

'I'm Alice and this is my cat Dinah,' said Alice. 'We've come to Wonderland to find a birthday party. Is it your birthday today?'

'No,' replied Tweedledum and Tweedledee. 'But we wish it was. We're fed up of fighting. May we come with you to find a party?'

'Certainly,' said Alice.
'Meow!' said Dinah.

So Alice and Dinah and Tweedledum and Tweedledee
set off together.

Before long they reached the Mad Hatter's tea party.

'I'm Alice and this is my cat Dinah,' said Alice. 'We've come to Wonderland to find a birthday party. Is it your birthday today?'

The Dormouse popped his nose out of the teapot. 'I never have a birthday,' he squeaked.

'You have one every year,' said the Mad Hatter firmly. 'But you are always fast asleep, so you never notice.' And he tried to put the lid back on the teapot.

'I would love to see a real birthday cake,' squeaked the Dormouse. 'May we come with you to find a birthday party?'

'Certainly,' said Alice.

'Meow!' said Dinah.

So Alice and Dinah and Tweedledum and Tweedledee and the Mad Hatter and the March Hare and the Dormouse, all set off together.

Before long they reached the Red Queen's Palace.

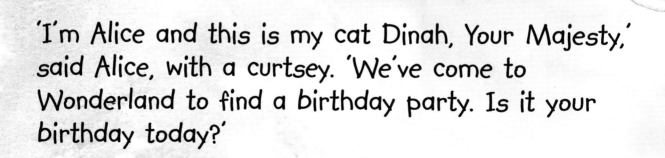

'I'm Alice and this is my cat Dinah, Your Majesty,' said Alice, with a curtsey. 'We've come to Wonderland to find a birthday party. Is it your birthday today?'

The tall Red Queen looked down at Alice and her friends.

'It's not my birthday,' she said. 'But of course a Queen wears her party clothes every day.
May I come with you to find a birthday party?'

'Certainly,' said Alice.

'Meow!' said Dinah.

So Alice and Dinah and Tweedledum and Tweedledee and the Mad Hatter and the March Hare and the Dormouse and the tall Red Queen all set off together.

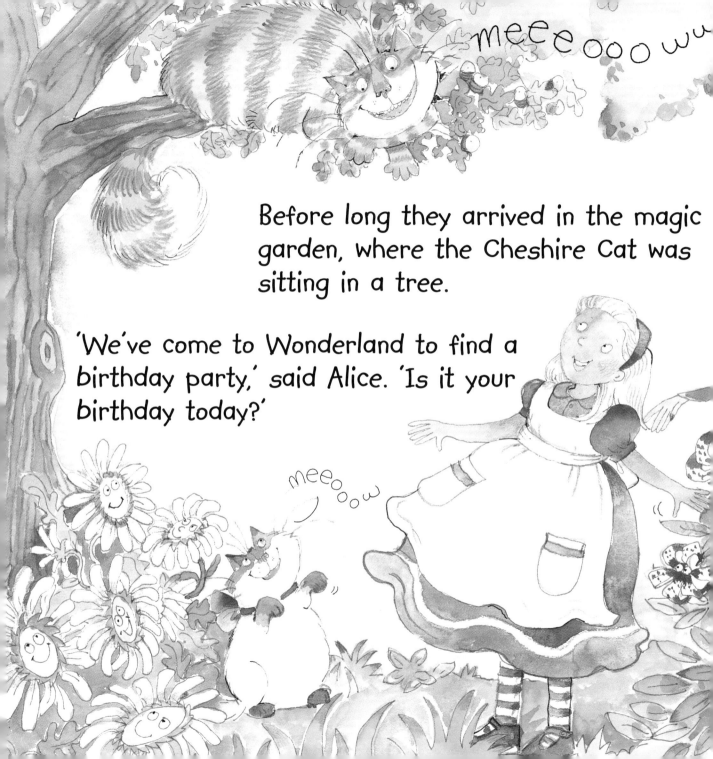

meeeooo wu

Before long they arrived in the magic garden, where the Cheshire Cat was sitting in a tree.

'We've come to Wonderland to find a birthday party,' said Alice. 'Is it your birthday today?'

meeooow

The Cheshire Cat meowed very loudly and Dinah meowed back. 'It's not my birthday,' grinned the Cheshire Cat, 'But your cat Dinah has just told me it's her birthday today, so of course we must have a surprise birthday party – Dinah's birthday party!'

They gave Dinah a Wonderland birthday party, with balloons and presents and ice-cream and a big birthday cake.

'Dinah,' laughed Alice, 'Why didn't you tell me it was your birthday?'

'Meow!'
said Dinah.

meeoow

Alice and Dinah
New Tales from Wonderland

Humpty Dumpty's Magic Garden

One afternoon Alice
looked at her bedroom and said to
her cat, Dinah, 'This bedroom is very
untidy. You must help me tidy up.'

Alice and Dinah worked very hard. They put the toys back in their boxes. They placed the books back on the shelves. They folded Alice's clothes neatly in the drawers.

Everything looked clean and tidy. Except the
plant on the window ledge. It did not look tidy
at all. It looked very sad and raggedy.

'Oh, Dinah,' said Alice, 'The poor plant looks so sad and raggedy. I don't know how to make it better.'

Dinah leaped up onto the window ledge and sniffed at the plant. She did not know how to make it better either.

Alice had an idea. 'Let's take the plant to
Wonderland,' she said. 'Someone there will
know just what to do to make it feel better.'

She picked up the raggedy plant and ran to the meadow. Dinah rushed after her.

Hidden away under the hedge was a secret rabbit hole which led to Alice and Dinah's Wonderland.

Alice popped into the hole.

Down,
 down,
  down
 she
   fell.
     Down,
       down,
        down
         fell
       Dinah,
         close
          behind
            her.

BUMP!
Alice landed
first.

BUMP!
Dinah landed
second.

'Careful!' said a rather cross voice. 'If you land on me I will break and who will put me together again?'

'Goodness, it's Humpty Dumpty!' exclaimed Alice.

'Please, Mr Dumpty, our plant is very sad and raggedy. Do you know anyone in Wonderland who can make it better?'

'We will ask some of my friends,' he replied.

First, Humpty Dumpty took them to the kitchen, where the cook was making soup.

'Can you make my plant better?' asked Alice.

'I can't make it better,' replied the cook. 'Let me cook it in this delicious soup.'

'How horrid!' said Alice, and hurried away as fast as she could.

Humpty Dumpty took them to meet some more of his friends. One was a Queen with a red crown. One was a Queen with a white crown.

'Can you make my plant better, your Majesties?' asked Alice.

'Yes we can,' they replied together. 'What you must do is ...'

But before they could give Alice the answer they both fell fast asleep and started to snore loudly.

'How silly!' said Alice with a big sigh.

Then Humpty Dumpty led Alice and Dinah into a garden full of bright flowers.

'This is my magic garden,' said Humpty Dumpty. 'All the flowers in this garden can talk.'

'Then they can tell me how to make my plant better,' said Alice happily.

The flowers nodded their heads at Alice.

'Your plant is thirsty,' they said.
'Give it a drink of water and it
will soon feel better.'

A magic watering can came sailing through the air and gave the plant a refreshing drink.

The little plant lifted up its head and smiled.

'Oh, thank you watering can. Thank you flowers. Thank you Humpty Dumpty,' cried Alice.

'Wonderland is the best place in the whole wide world.'

Alice and Dinah,
New Tales from Wonderland

The Mad Hatter's Striped Pyjamas

Alice looked at the rain trickling down the window and said to Dinah, 'We can't play outside today; it's too wet. What shall we do instead?'

Dinah was already having fun, making silly faces at herself in Alice's long mirror.

Alice went to the mirror and peered into it. 'I always look exactly the same,' she said to Dinah, 'And so do you. Shall we play at dressing-up and try on lots of different clothes?'

They looked in all
the cupboards...

...and drawers.

They looked on top
of the wardrobe...

...and under the bed. But they couldn't find any different clothes. All Alice's dresses looked exactly the same.

'Let's go to Wonderland,' said Alice.
'Everybody there wears very odd clothes.'

So they ran as fast as they could, through the rain, and jumped into the secret rabbit hole which leads down to Alice's Wonderland.

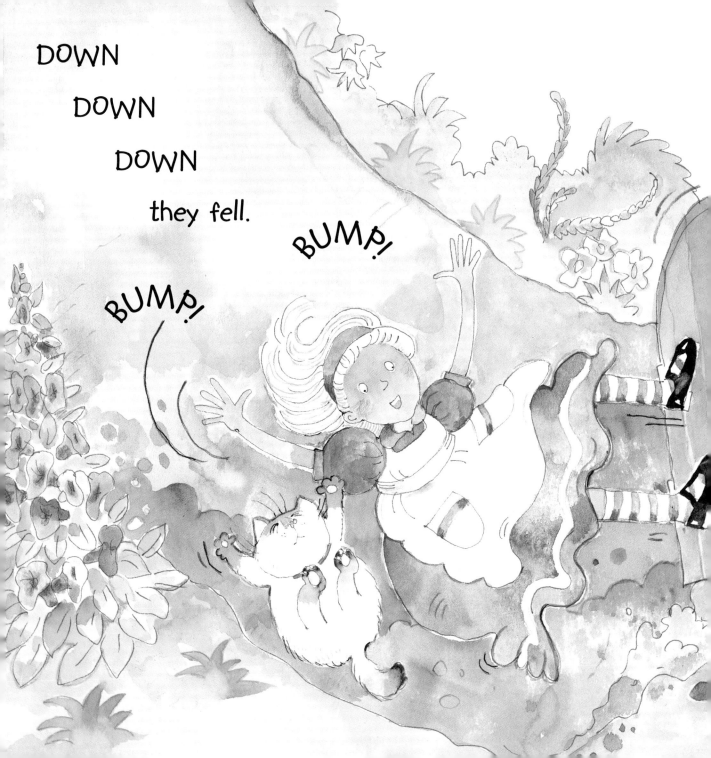

They landed right next to the Mad Hatter.
He was very surprised to see them.

'Mad Hatter,' said Alice, 'We don't have any clothes for dressing-up. Can you help us?'

'Of course! Of course!' replied the Mad Hatter, and
he gave Alice his hat to try on. But it was far too big.

Then he tried the hat on Dinah.
But it was far too big for her, too!

'No good! No good!' said the Mad Hatter, as he put his hat back on his head. 'Let's ask the caterpillar.'

The Mad Hatter held onto Alice's hand and Dinah's paw. He ran so fast that their feet didn't touch the ground.

They found the caterpillar snoozing on top of a mushroom. He opened one eye, gave a huge yawn and said, 'Who are you?'

Alice stood on tiptoe and peeped over the edge of the
mushroom. 'I'm Alice,' she replied. 'We don't have any
dressing-up clothes. Can you help us?'

'I only wear shoes,' said the caterpillar, 'You may try them if you wish.' Alice saw he was wearing lots and lots of tiny shoes, one for each of his tiny feet.

Alice and Dinah tried to put on the shoes but their feet were far too big. 'No good! No good!' said the Mad Hatter, 'Let's ask the Clothes Horse; she washes all our clothes. She has just washed my pyjamas.'

The Clothes Horse was standing in a field having a cup of tea with the Bread-and-butter-fly.

She was covered in all sorts of wonderful clothes which were drying in the warm sunshine.

Alice and Dinah and the Mad Hatter tried on all the funny hats. They tried on all the funny coats and all the funny shoes and socks. But Alice saved her favourite costume till last. Can you guess what it was?

The Mad Hatter's striped pyjamas, of course!

'This is my best dressing-up party ever,' laughed Alice. 'I always have the most fun in Wonderland.'

The White Rabbit's Red Nose

'ATISHOOO!!' Alice sneezed *very* loudly.
Dinah, the cat, jumped in the air with surprise.

Alice blew her nose on a big white handkerchief and sneezed again, very, *very* loudly, `A-A-A-ATISHOOO!!!'

'Oh dear!' said Alice, 'I've caught a cold.
I wish someone knew how to make it better.'

Dinah stood by the door and meowed. 'Of course,' said Alice, 'We'll go and ask our friends in Wonderland. You are a clever cat, Dinah.'

They ran as fast as they could to the secret
rabbit hole which leads to Alice and Dinah's
Wonderland. Alice jumped in first. Dinah followed
close behind.

DOWN
   DOWN
      DOWN
         they fell.

As they arrived in Wonderland
Alice heard an *enormous*
sneeze - `A-A-A-ATISHOOO!!!!!!`

She turned round and saw the White Rabbit. He had a bright red nose.

'I have a very bad cold,' said the White Rabbit, shaking his head sadly, 'and my pink nose has turned red.'

'Poor White Rabbit,' said Alice, tucking her arm through his, 'Let's find someone in Wonderland who can make us both better again.'

First they went to visit the Cook in her kitchen.

'The Cook makes good, hot soup,' said the White Rabbit, 'Perhaps that will make us better.'

But the Cook was shaking pepper into the soup. As she waved her giant pepper pot in the air, all the pepper flew about and *everyone* began to sneeze - even Dinah.

ATISHOOO! ATISHOOO!! ATISHOOO!!! ATISHOOO!!!!

`That hasn't helped my cold at all,' said Alice crossly.

Atishooo...

Atishooo!

Next they went to visit the Mad Hatter at his tea party.

'The Mad Hatter makes good strong tea,' said the White Rabbit, 'Perhaps that will make us better.'

But the Dormouse had got stuck in the teapot again.
He was singing `Twinkle Twinkle Little Star' and waving
his legs in the air.

`We shan't be able to get any tea here,' said the
White Rabbit.

As they walked on through the magic garden the Cheshire Cat suddenly appeared in one of the trees. 'The White Rabbit and I have caught very bad colds,' said Alice. 'Can you help us get better?'

'*You* haven't caught a cold.' said the Cheshire Cat, with a wide grin, 'The cold has caught *you*. I can disappear so colds can never catch *me*.'

When they looked up again he had vanished
completely, and was nowhere to be seen.
`Curiouser and curiouser,' said Alice.

Around the corner came the jolly March Hare
`Can you make our colds better?' said Alice
and the White Rabbit together.

'The best thing for making colds better,' chuckled the March Hare, 'is lots of tickling.'

And he chased them round and round the magic garden, tickling them with long pieces of straw.

Everybody laughed and laughed until at last they all fell over in a big heap.

They laughed so loudly that the Mad Hatter, the Dormouse and the Cook came to see what was going on.

And the Cheshire cat
appeared again to watch the fun.

'Listen,' shouted Alice, 'I've stopped sneezing.'

'Look,' shouted the White Rabbit, 'my nose is pink again.'

Their colds were completely better.

'Yes,' said Alice, 'everything's better in Wonderland.'